WAITING FOR BABY

For Debbie, Kelsey, and Amy—my joy
T.B.

Many thanks to Mark, Maureen, Carol,
Susan, and Kevin
L.L.

Library of Congress Cataloging-in-Publication Data
Birdseye, Tom.
Waiting for baby / by Tom Birdseye ;
illustrated by Loreen Leedy.—1st ed.
p.   cm.
Summary: A child eargerly awaits the arrival
of a new baby in the family.
ISBN 0-8234-0892-2
[1. Babies—Fiction. 2. Brothers and sisters—Fiction.]
I. Leedy, Loreen, ill. II. Title.
PZ7.B5213Wai   1991   90-29076   CIP   AC
[E]—dc20

WAITING FOR BABY

by Tom Birdseye
illustrated by Loreen Leedy

Holiday House / New York

Hello, Baby.
It's light where I am.
The wind is rustling the leaves, then gliding through the window,
and brownies are fresh out of the oven.

Soon you'll be here, Baby,
together with me.
I'm waiting, waiting,
waiting for you.

We'll play together,
hide-and-seek in the closet,
after we build a city of blocks.

Throwing sticks will be fun with Maggie.
She'll fetch,
then drop them at our feet and beg for more.

You and I will hug sometimes.
Or roll-rough and tumble,
laughing and giggling on the living-room floor.

When I show you my favorite toys—
my butterfly net,
my alphabet puzzle,
that wooden train with the broken wheel—
we'll be family.

Soon you'll be here, Baby,
together with me.
I'm waiting, waiting,
waiting for you.

I'll help you pick out clothes to wear,
and tuck in your shirttail just like mine.

We can play dress-up too.
We'll be super kids!
Our capes will fly as we save the day.

We can make a fort under the table.

I'll read to you—
Stories! Stories! Stories!
I love books.
I think you will too.

Maybe we'll swing side by side,
reaching for the sun with our toes.

Or ride our bikes down the driveway and back.
Vroom! Beep Beep! Let's go!

You'll lie on the grass and stare at the stars with me.
The moon, when it's full, has a face.
We'll sing songs about pizza and pigs,
and laugh at things—
you and I.

Soon you'll be here, Baby,
together with me.
I'm waiting, waiting,
waiting for you.

We'll paint at my easel—
rainbows, rockets, and smoke from house chimneys.

We can pick strawberries.
Red juice will get on our faces.

Next we'll go into the bath.
We'll swim through boats and bubbles.
I'll scrub your back and you'll scrub mine.

We'll have milk and cookies
before pajamas and bed.
Then, we'll climb up the stairs,
teddy bears under our arms.

I'll tell you a secret.
You'll tell me one too,
because we'll be friends.

There's something special
in being together.
We know that.

Soon you'll be here, Baby,
together with me.
I'm waiting, waiting,
waiting for you.

Now you're here, Baby!
You're so much smaller than I'd thought you'd be.

But I'm holding you.
And I'm loving you.

Because you're finally, *finally*
together with me.

DATE			